Molly Moonshine
and the
Tooth Fairy's Wand

Richard Hamilton

Illustrated by Jan Nesbitt

CollinsChildren'sBooks
An imprint of HarperCollinsPublishers

First published in Great Britain by
CollinsChildren'sBooks 1996

1 3 5 7 9 8 6 4 2

CollinsChildren'sBooks is an imprint of
HarperCollins*Publishers* Ltd,
77-85 Fulham Palace Road,
Hammersmith, London W6 8JB

Printed and bound in Great Britain
by Caledonian International Book Manufacturing Ltd, Glasgow G64

ISBN HB 0 00 185669 3
ISBN PB 0 00 675254 3

Chapter 1

Molly Moonshine lost a tooth. It wasn't a very big tooth – only about the size of a pea – but it was important. Because on Friday her smile looked like this...

And on Saturday it looked like this...

It felt funny too. Molly pushed her tongue into the gap. It felt soft and strange. A bit like a tasteless banana.

"Never mind," said her mother.
"You can put the tooth under your
pillow tonight. Then the tooth fairy
will come and take it away."

"What will she do with it?" asked Molly.

Her mother thought. "I'm not sure," she said, "but the tooth fairy always leaves something behind."

"What?" asked Molly, who was always asking questions.

"I don't know. You'll have to wait and see."

"What does the tooth fairy look like?"

"Nobody knows," said her mother, "because she comes in the middle of the night."

"Why?"

"Because that's when you're asleep."

"But I want to see her."

"Well, she's busy. She's a busy
fairy and *I'm* a busy mother, Molly
Moonshine. *You* are a little
chatterbox. Now run along, I'd
like some peace and quiet."

Molly sighed. "But Mum, I don't like peace and quiet – I like *talking*."

Chapter 2

That night, Molly placed the tooth under her pillow. She tried to stay awake because she really wanted to see the tooth fairy. Perhaps she could even talk to the tooth fairy.

Molly tried saying her alphabet backwards in her head, so that she would stay awake. But it was no use. As she was saying it she fell asleep.

When she woke up it was morning.

The first thing Molly did in the
morning was to lift up her pillow
and look underneath.

The tooth was no longer there!
The tooth fairy had been. She had
taken Molly's tooth away!

Molly felt very excited. The tooth
had gone—

But there was nothing under the
pillow.

At first Molly was disappointed.

Then she was cross! How could the fairy take her tooth but forget to leave something? It was a good clean tooth, too. Molly *always* cleaned her teeth properly.

Then she saw something under the bed.

It was a small, dark stick. It was
like a pencil with a shiny, silver tip.
Molly stared at it.

Was it…?
Could it be…?

She felt her heart beat faster. She
knew what it was. She knew
exactly what it was.
It was the tooth fairy's wand!

Chapter 3

Molly dressed and rushed
downstairs to breakfast at record
speed.

In the kitchen, her mother was cooking the lunch *and* eating breakfast at the same time!

Her father was reading the
newspaper *and* doing up his
shoelaces at the same time.

"Guess what?" Molly said. "The tooth fairy came in the night!"

Molly's mother stopped chopping onions for a moment. "Oh, I'm sorry—"

"She left me her wand!" Molly whispered very loudly.

Her mother's eyes widened. "Did she? Oh good." She smiled and started chopping onions again.

After breakfast, Molly took the little
wand out into the garden. She
held it up in the air and stroked it.

"Abracadabra," she said,
waving the wand round.

Nothing happened.
She tried to say it again in a
magical, mysterious way.
"Aaaaabracadabraaaa!"

But again nothing happened.
"Speak to me!" she ordered the
wand.

Then something *did* happen.
Something completely amazing.
The wand moved. It twisted in her
hand. Then suddenly, it slipped
from between her fingers like a
wet bar of soap.

It landed on the ground and bounced up and down the garden path. And as it did so, it sang:

"Did you ever talk to a stork?
Or try to speak to a leek?
Have you ever had a laugh with a giraffe?
Or a chat with a little pussycat?"

Molly stared at the wand. She wasn't quite sure what to say, except "No," which she did.

"Well, in that case, I can help,"
said the wand, jumping back into
her hand. "Because I can do
something special. *I can make
things talk.* Animals, plants, toys,
tents or teapots. Just point me at
something and say the words
'Chit-chat-chatterbox!' That thing
will talk until you say STOP."

"STOP," said Molly.

Chapter 4

The wand fell silent. Molly's heart
was racing. She knew immediately
who she wanted to talk to: Raggy,
her favourite toy. She rushed
inside to find him.

Raggy was a rabbit who sat by the window in Molly's bedroom.

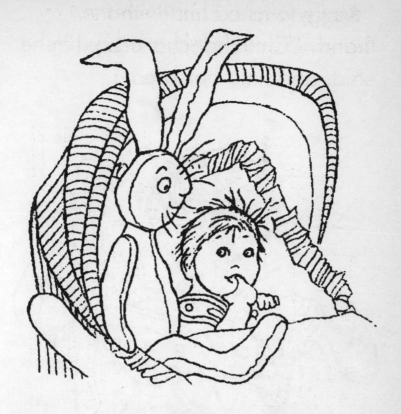

He was given to Molly when she
was a baby. He was beautiful
then. He was clean and perfect.
Now his nose was worn out, his
ears were patched and he only
had two-and-a-half whiskers.

Molly touched him with the
wand. "Chit-chat-chatterbox!" she
said, and held her breath.

Raggy stiffened. His little nose
twitched. His two-and-a-half
whiskers bristled. One eye
opened.

"Hello," said Molly.

Raggy's mouth opened and shut.
He smiled. He had two big front
teeth which Molly had never seen
before.

"Hellooooo, Molly," he said,
very slowly.

"Do you remember the very first time you saw me?" asked Molly.

Raggy folded his paws in front of his little tummy and began to speak. He told Molly all about his arrival soon after she was born. How he sat near her cot and watched her sleep.

Then he told her about the day
he was taken for a walk and fell in
a puddle. And how he was put in
the washing machine.

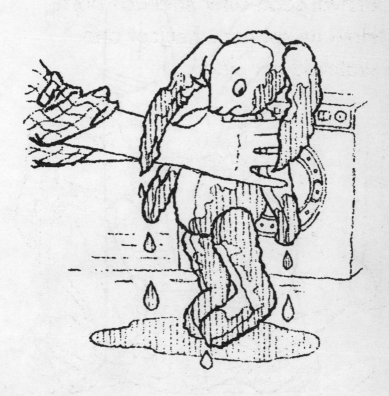

He told her about the time he lost his whiskers. They were caught in a door and snapped off.

He told her about the dog that
ran away with him in his mouth.

Raggy talked and talked and
talked! Molly could hardly believe
it. He talked even more than *she*
did!

"Can you imagine what it's like to be stuck in a dark cellar, unable to cry out, unable to move?" Raggy asked Molly after a story about a toy tea party.

"Er... no," said Molly, who had been looking out of the window.

"You dropped me down the stairs and I fell into a dark corner. I was stuck between a spider's web and a mouse hole."

"Oh, creepy!" Molly shivered.

"The spider crawled over me and fixed his web to one of my paws. The mouse pulled all my stuffing out! Luckily your mum found me and mended me."

"Well, I promise—"
Molly was about to promise that
it would never happen again,
when outside her bedroom door
she heard her father shouting.

"Molly!"

"STOP!" she cried as he turned the door handle.

But it was too late. Her father burst into the room.

"What are you doing? It's nearly lunchtime. We've been calling you for ages!"

"I'm coming." Molly looked at Raggy. He had fallen off the window sill. He lay on the carpet.

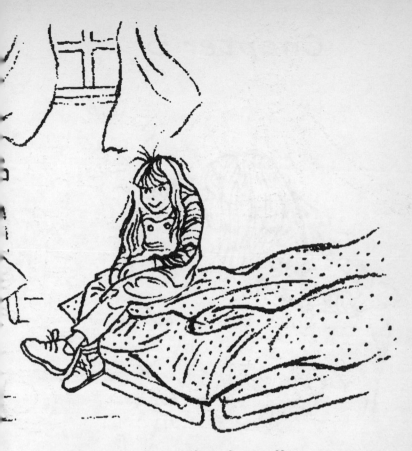

He was completely still.

Of course! Molly had said the magic word. Raggy wouldn't talk anymore.

Chapter 5

Molly spent the rest of the weekend talking. She talked to toys and flowers. She talked to bookends and dolls. She talked to the pigs on her wallpaper.

She even talked to a carrot!

It might have been because she talked so much...
Or it might have been a very chewy toffee...

But on Sunday afternoon Molly found that she had *another* loose tooth. She touched it, she wiggled it, she tapped it (she knew she shouldn't), and suddenly it fell out into her hand. Then she had a *brilliant* idea. She would talk to her tooth!

She rushed upstairs and picked
up the tooth fairy's wand.
"Chit-chat-chatterbox!" she said,
pointing at the tooth.

The tooth whistled. It was a short,
bright whistle that made Molly
jump.

"Good afternoon, Molly Moonshine! Pleased to meet you," the tooth said merrily. It did a little twirl on the palm of Molly's hand.

"Shhh! I didn't think a tooth could make so much noise," said Molly.

"Noise?" said the tooth. "Are you saying I'm noisy?"

"No, no" said Molly quickly. She didn't want to upset the tooth. "It's just that for something so small you're quite... loud."

"Well that's because there's always so much talk round us teeth, that we have to shout or we can't hear each other."

"Do you mean teeth talk to each other?" asked Molly.

"Oh yes – we chatter all the time. Almost as much as you, Molly Moonshine. Chat, chat, chat. Morning, noon and night."

Molly felt her teeth with her
tongue. Were they all chattering
now? It was hard to imagine.

"Can you tell me about the tooth
fairy?" she asked.

"The tooth fairy? Ah." There was a pause. "What do you want to know?"

"Will she come tonight?"
"Of course. Put me under your pillow and she'll come and take me away."
"Where to?" asked Molly.

"To the place where old teeth go."

"What time will the tooth fairy come?" asked Molly.

"It's hard to tell. She has a lot to do in one night."

"Do you mean there's only one tooth fairy?"

"Only one. Just like there's only
one Father Christmas."

"And will she take her magic
wand back?" Molly closed her
eyes. She didn't really want to
know the answer.

"Of course," replied the tooth.

"The wand is only left when you lose your first tooth. And only if you're the first person the tooth fairy visits that night. First person, first tooth. Funny that. You've got to be very lucky..."

The tooth continued to talk, but Molly wasn't listening. She was thinking about the wand. She didn't want to lose it. But then she couldn't think of anything else she wanted to talk to. In fact, she was quite tired of talking.

"STOP!" she said to the tooth.

"Bathtime!" called her mother.

Chapter 6

That night, Molly lay in the dark wondering when the tooth fairy would come. Under her pillow lay her tooth *and* the tooth fairy's wand.

I'll pretend to be asleep, Molly thought, closing her eyes. If I'm lucky I'll see the tooth fairy taking my tooth.

But she forgot to pretend... and she fell asleep.

In the morning, the first thing
Molly did was to feel under her
pillow. There, she found a shiny
new coin. Her tooth had gone. So
had the wand.

Molly lay in her bed and listened... to nothing. Her bedroom was quiet, it was lovely. She could think about so many things. Now she understood what Mum meant by peace and quiet.

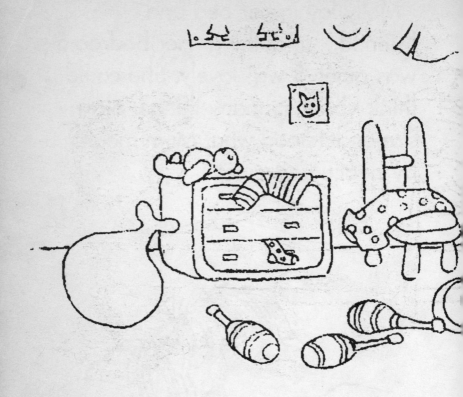

"Are you awake, Molly?" her
mother called.

"Yes," called Molly quietly.

"Did the tooth fairy come?"
asked her mother.

"Yes, she did," Molly whispered.

Molly's mother came into her
bedroom. She frowned. "Are you
all right, Molly Moonshine?"
"Shhh, Mum!" said Molly. "I'm
enjoying the peace and quiet!"